Love Potion No 9

Chapter One

It's Not in the Cards

'*I'm SO sorry!*'

Bethany was shutting down her computer to leave work when the text was received. She'd been counting down the minutes until five to rush home and get ready for tonight. Dinner and a movie with one of her friends might not seem exciting, but she couldn't face spending another Friday night alone thinking about all the fun Mark was having without her.

His new girlfriend, the homewrecker he left her for, was everywhere now. Not really, but Bethany saw reminders of her everywhere she went. The scent of lavender and all shades of purple brought back rushing scenes of the night she caught them in bed. Every blonde ponytail she saw was that slut running out of the house she and Mark had shared, scared Bethany might come after her.

If she didn't do something normal soon, something more than eat take out while sitting on her couch binge watching a series, she was going to lose it. Tiff had been her key to unlocking something fun, but as soon as she saw the text, she knew the key didn't fit the lock.

'*Brad's family came into town unexpectedly...*'

The notification appeared on the screen, but Bethany ignored it. She didn't need to read the whole message to figure out Tiff was canceling on her last minute.

Her feet moved slower on the way to the elevator. There was no reason to hurry when she'd be spending the night alone, again, with only her broken heart to keep her company.

All of her friends said the quickest way to get over someone was with someone new. Bethany had heard it before, but she was too shy to get back out there. Dating had never been easy for her. Trying to sell herself and what she could bring to a relationship always made her feel fake. It wasn't so bad before she met Mark. Almost all of her friends were on the hunt with her. In the four years she wasted with him, they all went off the market. Most were married, two were expecting their first child, and the rest were living with someone.

Then there was Bethany. She was the scratched up floor model tucked away in the back room.

"Stop it." She told her steering wheel as she got into the car.

There was a voice mail from Tiff which she played before backing out of her parking spot. "Hey, girl! I really am sorry! I'll make it up to you. I promise!! Please promise me you'll still go out tonight. Please! Just go to a bar and order one drink. See what happens. Even if you go straight home after, at least you got out and on your own. I'll talk to you later. I love you, girl!"

Bethany began the five minute drive home. As she neared her turn, she passed the psychic house. Even when she lived with Mark, this house was on her way to work. She'd been driving by it every day for almost seven years since she started her job. No one she knew had ever stopped there, but it had a lot of business. There were always different cars in the parking lot when the open sign was lit up.

Bethany considered checking it out, but drove right on past instead. There had been a few other times she thought about it too. Mostly she was tempted when she was single or trying to figure out what was going wrong in her relationships.

The car had a mind of its own, circling around the block, and bringing her back to the psychic house. *'Why not?'* she thought. *'At least I can say I did go somewhere when Tiff asks.'*

It was an ordinary house tucked between businesses on the busy main road. There were a handful of homes nestled between corner stores, ice cream shops and places that sold second hand video games. This one had a screened in front porch blasting the street with neon signs reading "Tarot" and "Psychic."

The parking lot wasn't much more than an expanded driveway. It could hold about four cars at a time, and right now, there were only two besides hers. She didn't see another door other than the one on the side of the porch, but there was nothing on it saying "Enter." With a deep breath, she forced herself out of the car. As she approached the door, a man who appeared to be in his forties walked out. He held the door open for her, but avoided making eye contact. Once she was on the porch, he practically ran to his car before anyone else could spot him.

A gruff sounding voice said, "So you want to fall in love?"

Bethany looked to see where it had originated. An older woman was standing at the door to the house. She was wearing an unflattering dress and had hair as dark as night. It was either dyed or a wig because the wrinkled, sun spotted skin on her face was proof her hair should be snow white.

'It's Friday night, and I'm meeting with a psychic instead of going out. It's not hard to assume I'm single.'

Inside the house, the front room was exactly how you'd expect to find the home of any woman old enough to be a grandmother. The layout was perfectly arranged. Everything was neat and orderly. The only glaring difference was the white folding table in the center of the room and a bookshelf with items for sale.

They sat down, and the psychic who introduced herself as Max, immediately asked for payment. "Cash or card only. No checks."

Once her card was approved, the woman dealt a series of cards from a tarot deck onto the table. Some of them had familiar sounding names, but the only one Bethany would remember later was "Cups." Throughout the reading, Max had a lot to say about Bethany's career. There was a lot of success in her future with raises and promotions. She should also expect a big move, but didn't specify if it was work related or not. There wasn't a single detail mentioned about her love life.

The reading was wrapping up, so Bethany asked, "What about my love life?"

"Sorry," Max said. "It's not in the cards today. That doesn't mean love isn't in your future. It is; I'm sure of it. The cards just felt there were more important things to discuss. Maybe next time."

'Of course,' Bethany felt like she'd been had. *'Next time. Avoid the only thing I was curious about to ensure my return to see if there's better luck then.'* She was mad at herself for wasting the money. The whole set up was little more than a gimmick to scam people.

Max stood up to show her out saying, "Not all men are like Mark. Don't lose hope."

That name made Bethany freeze. She was pushing her chair back to stand, and it almost toppled when she stopped moving.

The psychic laughed at her reaction. "That fixed those negative thoughts about me, didn't it? There's a reason all real psychics aren't rich from predicting winning lottery numbers. We can't always choose the information which comes through. Tools like tarot cards helps in our divination, but it doesn't give us the key to being all knowing."

Bethany felt even more out of place. Somehow this woman had been able to tell what she was thinking. She wanted to apologize, but wasn't ready to admit it either.

She looked around at the items on display. There were a number of trinkets like crystals and various gems. There were candles in various sizes with a note reading there was more in the back. Ask about specific colors and sizes. A number of vials lined the top shelf with small tags hanging from their neck. "Moon water?" she mumbled out loud.

"It helps with spell work. I charge some every full moon and make sure there's enough to keep stocked here."

"You're a witch?' The words rolled out easily. It was a growing trend according to a friend of hers who was not a witch, but seemed to be an expert on the subject. She carried crystals and talked about chakras like other people clutched rosary beads and prayed.

Max said, "That's how I know my cards." She shrugged like it was no big deal, and she didn't want to talk about it. "If I advertise that detail on my sign, I'd have no customers," she added.

There was a beautiful glass bottle catching Bethany's eye. It was tear drop shaped with a gold neck. The cork topper was decorated in miniature flowers and a tiny witch's hat sat on top. The liquid inside was dark, but it sparkled in the light. The tag hanging from it read, "Love Potion No. 9." Bethany giggled and set it back down.

"There is nothing funny about that potion," Max said sternly.

"It can't be serious. What is it? Like a perfume with pheromones in it or something?" She had tried those perfumes with mixed results. Men didn't come running, but it gave her a confidence boost which did turn some heads.

"No," Max said slowly, moving closer. "It's a potion. Says so in the name. You drink it not wear it."

Bethany turned the tag over and saw the price. *'Three hundred dollars!'* Her eyes widened, and her mouth dropped. *'For that little bottle? It's probably a one-time use too. That's ridiculous.'*

"It's guaranteed to work," Max said. She moved the bottle back away from Bethany. "Or your money back."

"How do you know if it works?"

"Oh, you'll know," Max chuckled.

Bethany shook her head. "No, how do *you* know? What if someone returns it and lies about it?"

"In all my years, I've never had a complaint. That's how I know."

It was still tempting her. She wondered if there was a discounted price to try it. Max was trying to shoo her out because another customer was waiting. *'Fuck it,'* Bethany thought. "I'll buy it."

The grin on Max's face said she was expecting this. She wrapped the bottle carefully in tissue and tucked it into a box perfect for its size. After running Bethany's credit card for the second time, she doled out the instructions. "Alright, sweetie, you must be very careful with it. You only need a couple drops.

Put it in your drink, sprinkle it on your eggs. Doesn't matter."

"It tastes disgusting, so don't say I didn't warn you. I wouldn't drink it straight if I were you."

Max handed the box over. "One more thing: only use it when you're sure of the person you want to attract. Don't use it all the time. You don't want the wrong kind of attention."

Bethany nodded and looked at the box. Buyer's remorse was already settling in, but Max didn't give off the impression she accepted refunds. "Got it. A couple drops. Tastes gross. Mix it with something. Use when certain."

"Hmm," Max said, narrowing her eyes. One corner of her mouth screwed back, and she crossed her arms. It seemed like she wasn't confident in the sale either. Finally, she exhaled and relaxed. "If you have any questions, stop back by. I'm happy to help."

"Okay. Thanks!" Bethany said, hurrying out the door before the old woman could add anything else.

The whole drive home she berated herself for being an idiot. It was probably nothing more than molasses. A trick to take advantage of people like her, and it clearly worked. The moment her hand was on the door Max probably pulled another bottle from her pocket for the next customer. *'The bottle was pretty though,'* she thought. She'd definitely find a purpose to reuse it. *'Not three hundred dollars pretty though.'*

She pulled into the parking lot for her apartment building and checked her phone. Not one single notification. This was her life. She was a couple of cats away from being crazy and destined to be alone forever. Picking up the box, she decided to take Tiff's advice and go out, trying out the potion in the process. It wouldn't work, but it sure beat staying at home holding nothing but a remote control.

Chapter Two

Revenge Served Cold

Bethany made the decision to have one drink. She'd sit at the bar slowly sipping her bottle to see if this potion did anything for her at all. If there were no bites by the end of one beer, she'd come back home. At least she'd be able to honestly tell Tiff she didn't spend her birthday sitting on the couch all night long.

When she finished getting ready to go out, she stared at the box, tapping her fingers on the sides. *It's not going to work. You're an idiot.*

For three hundred dollars, she wasn't going to let it sit and collect dust in a closet either. She removed the bottle, admiring again how beautiful it looked. The cork stopper was decorated so exquisitely, and she took care to remove it without destroying the accents. As soon as it was out, the smell hit her.

It smelled rancid. Bethany turned her head and coughed. Her eyes watered, and her stomach twisted and flopped in response. She gently put the cork back into place and left the bathroom for some fresh air.

She walked toward the kitchen lecturing herself, carrying the bottle with her. "Three hundred dollars! You're drinking it."

A couple drops didn't seem like it would be enough to work. She opened the refrigerator and her cabinets trying to find something to eat with it. Mixing it with a drink probably wasn't a good idea because it would extend the amount of time she had to deal with getting it down her throat.

Bethany shut the last cabinet door and sighed. She opened a drawer and pulled out a teaspoon. "A spoonful should be enough to see how it works," she said, slamming the drawer shut. There was enough to try it at least ten times drinking it by the spoon. That should be enough to gauge results.

Her phone dinged and she glanced at the screen expecting to see Tiff's name in the notification box. The text was from Mark. She froze. A mixture of fear and excitement flowed through her, and she wasn't sure if she wanted to read it.

Finally, she picked up her phone and clicked on it. He had a couple things of hers, including the remote for the television in her bedroom, and wanted to know if he could run them by her apartment. He was five minutes away.

"Yeah," she replied.

The screen lit up almost immediately with another text from him saying he expected her to be at home with no plans. *'Ouch.'*

It angered her and steeled her resolve to drink the rotted concoction in front of her. She opened the bottle again and poured a spoonful. It was thick like molasses and oozed onto the spoon. She breathed through her mouth to avoid getting sick before the spoon touched her lips.

The moment the liquid reached her mouth it was a battle to avoid throwing up. Her stomach reacted violently before it made its way down her throat. There were clear indications it was planning on ejecting this sludge from her body. Her mouth began watering in a defensive response, and her jaws clenched. The idea of vomiting close to fifty dollars' worth of toxic muck was almost harder to swallow than the potion.

Bethany tore into the loaf of bread on the counter grabbing several slices at once. She ripped them into pieces, shoving them in her mouth and chewing as fast as she could, swallowing it down to absorb the vile liquid. After a couple close calls, her stomach finally settled down.

It still made her feel sick just not in an urgent get to the bathroom way. *'What a waste! I'm not going to the bar feeling like this. There's no way I'm drinking alcohol on top of that.'* She'd just tell Tiff about Mark coming over and say it ruined her mood to go out. There was no way she was going to admit to the spontaneous purchase she made from a self-professed witch.

The sound of a car door slamming brought her attention to the window, and she looked out to see if Mark's car was parked on the street. She couldn't see it from her angle, but she did see a guy standing across the street, staring up at her. He waved at her and smiled like he'd been waiting for her to show her face. Then there was another man walking toward her building. He was yelling something at her she couldn't quite hear. And another. Then another. Within a minute, there were seven of them gathered nearby. They looked like cats gathered in an alley. Each time she looked at one, he'd grin, wave, yell something hopeful and try to catch her eye.

"That's weird," she muttered, slowly backing away from the window.

The knock on the door made her jump. Fight or flight was kicking in before she realized it was probably just Mark.

She walked to the door feeling thankful she had gone to the trouble of getting ready even if she wasn't going to wind up leaving the apartment. He could, and would, say whatever he wanted to, but she looked damn good.

The door swung open, and he burst into the hall carrying a small bag. "Wow!" His eyes widened, and he gazed at her, looking her up and down, with a lust in his eyes she'd never seen before.

"Mark?" She questioned when he did nothing more than stare.

He moved toward her as she walked backward away from him until she hit the back of her couch and had nowhere else to go. He pressed up against her, and said, "I want you."

Bethany shook her head and pushed against him, sliding with difficulty to get away from him. "Shouldn't you be with Chrissy?" The words were cold, but her body was not. She felt betrayed by herself the way she flushed, and the blood which pumped through her engorged her clit, showcased her heart beat between her legs and made her knees weak.

"Fuck Chrissy," he said, following her. "It's always been you. I want you, and I'll do anything to get you."

She was about to start screaming at him. They must've had a fight and now she was good enough for him again. *Like I've been sitting around waiting for him to come crawling back.'*

When she turned around to let him have it, she saw that look in his eyes again. She'd never seen such raw passion in him before. That's when she realized it was the potion. She glanced back at the bottle on the counter and decided to really test it out.

"Anything?"

Mark inched closer, and his hot breath exhaled on her neck. "Anything," he said in a raspy whisper.

"Take me home with you. Dump that whore, and you can have me."

He grabbed her hand and yanked her after him, leading her

out of the apartment. She was barely able to grab her purse and had to yell at him to stop so she could lock the door. He dragged her past the men waiting outside, screaming at them to back off. Once they were in his car, he sped to the house they used to share together. "Hurry," Bethany urged him on. "I can't wait much longer."

Chrissy shouted a slur of choice words as soon as they came inside. He screamed them right back, calling her every name in the book and ordering her to leave. This was *his* house after all, and if he wanted to make a fine point, Bethany's name was still on it as well. He was stripping down as they fought until he was naked telling her it was over. The woman ran from the home carrying a handful of what she could quickly grab. Mascara lines ran down her cheeks from her tears. Bethany couldn't help herself. She stood in the living room laughing as she watched the scene unfold.

Once the door was shut, Mark grabbed her. He wrapped one arm around her, lifting her up while planting his lips on top of hers. He began to walk her back to the bedroom they once shared, but she told him to stop. "Take me to the table. It's time for you to eat your dinner."

Mark grinned and did what she told him. He sat Bethany on the table, and began rubbing her mound over her jeans.

"Not so fast," she told him. "Work for it."

He put his hands on either side of her face and kissed her deeply. He hadn't been gentle like this with her for a long time before their breakup. His hands dropped to her breasts.

Bethany put her hand on the back of his head and held him in the kiss while his hands explored. Her breasts were firm and round. He squeezed them, cupped them, and pulled her shirt down to expose the cleavage protruding over her bra. He found her nipples through the thin lacy material, pinching them. He buried his head in them for a moment while Bethany giggled before she pushed him away.

Mark kept his mouth on her supple breasts while reaching down with his other hand, working on sliding her pants off. She let him struggle a minute before helping him. Once they were off, she spread her legs for him. "Mmm." Mark moaned, and bit his lower lip. His hand went to his own member, but Bethany reminded him, "Me first."

He nodded and brought his hands to her legs, lifting them over his shoulders. He leaned into her and licked the entire length of her folds.

"That's it," Bethany urged. "Be a good boy, and don't stop until you're told."

The words sent Mark into a frenzy. Either it turned him on, or he was in a race for her to take a turn pleasing him. He smashed his face into her, licking her. He lowered his head and licked her rim which caused her to scream, "Fuuuckkk!"

He stuck one finger inside her then two and began to fuck her quickly with his hand while licking her clit and teasing it gently with his lips. She'd never admit it to him, or anyone, but this was the first time she was getting laid since their breakup. It didn't take long for the first orgasm to relieve her body of the building frustration.

It encouraged him on, and he sucked on her clit. He brought his other hand into play, fingering her wet pussy and rubbing her clit with one while teasing her ass with the other. Mark obviously remembered how much she liked ass play. No man could forget something like that.

Several orgasms later, Bethany bent her legs at the knees and pulled them close enough to put her feet on his shoulders. She gently pushed him away. If this kept on any longer, she would fuck him tonight, and that was one thing she didn't want happening.

"Already," Mark grinned. The cocky bastard always believed he was god's gift in bed.

"Go on to the bedroom," she told him. "I'm going to clean up a bit then I'll join you."

Once he disappeared, Bethany jumped off the table and prayed her shaky legs wouldn't fail her. She dressed as quickly as she could and ordered and Uber with her phone for a pick up at the gas station two blocks away. She shut the door behind her as quietly as she could then practically sprinted there. While she waited for her ride, she blocked his number in her phone.

She'd never been so thankful to have a female driver, but the looks being cast her way in the rearview mirror told her the driver would be down if she said the word. At her building, she hurried to her apartment dodging several men asking for her number. She stepped inside and locked the door behind her. She wanted to jump up and down. She wanted to call someone, everyone. *'Tonight did NOT just happen!'* She had to settle for screaming into a pillow.

Right before she went to bed that night, she sent her friend Tiff a cryptic message. "Today was the best birthday I've ever had!" She followed the text with an eggplant emoji and three sweat droplet ones. Then she switched her phone to silent and laid it face down on her nightstand before falling fast asleep.

Chapter Three

Saturday

When Bethany opened her eyes Saturday morning, everything from the night before came rushing back. She stretched and grinned thinking about how Mark must feel this morning.

'Wait,' she sat up. *'How does he feel?'*

The potion obviously worked because Mark would've never acted in that manner otherwise. She never thought to ask Max how long the potion lasted. More importantly, how long will it affect the guy I'm with is what I need to know. *'It can't be too long,'* she thought. *'A day? At the most.'*

She took her phone with her to the bathroom, and it started vibrating in her hand halfway there. The screen showed a call from Tiff. "You can wait," she said, sending the call to voice mail.

When she finally made her way to the kitchen and started a pot of coffee, she checked her phone again. There were dozens of notifications, all from Tiff wondering what the hell happened. The last text was in all caps. "WHY WAS MARK CALLING ME IN THE MIDDLE OF THE NIGHT ASKING ABOUT YOU???"

Bethany cracked up laughing. This was too much. She sent a quick reply asking, "Come over?"

"Already on my way," Tiff replied.

Bethany was just finishing her toast and sliced orange she

decided on for breakfast when there was a knock at the door. As soon as Tiff walked into the apartment, she demanded, "Spill it! Now." She tried to appear angry, but couldn't keep her grin from showing.

"Oh my god!" Bethany squealed. "You won't believe it!"

The two friends sat at the table drinking coffee while Bethany filled her in on how she completely owned Mark the night before only leaving out the part about the psychic and her purchase. Tiff couldn't breathe from laughing so hard as Bethany described how he stripped in his living room in front of Chrissy while simultaneously dumping her and ordering her out of the house.

"So wait... You're not back together?" Tiff was confused when Bethany told her how she slipped out and left him hanging.

"Hell, no," Bethany said, getting a refill.

"What was last night about then? I don't understand."

"Revenge." The word tasted a little sour, but Bethany owned it. "Serves Chrissy right for what she did to me."

Tiff looked around the kitchen and dining area of the apartment. Something was on her mind. "I just don't understand. He was treating you like crap. I mean don't get me wrong. I'm glad he got his, but I'm trying to figure out how it happened."

The potion was still on the counter from the night before, and Bethany wasn't sure how Tiff would react if she told her about it. This was her best friend however. With a sigh, Bethany began, "There is one more thing."

She admitted to going to the psychic, the potion, all of it. When she was done, she watched her friend admire the bottle.

Tiff arched one eyebrow. "And you think this really works?"

"Well, I don't think last night would've happened otherwise," Bethany said with a shrug. "Do you?"

Her friend chewed her lower lip then broke out in a large smile and shook her head. "No, definitely not."

"When did he call you?" Bethany asked.

"Half the night!" Tiff pulled out her phone. "Let's see. He sent a text around midnight asking if I knew where you were."

'That's around the time I got home. He had probably been trying my phone for a while.'

"Ummm," Tiff was scrolling through her. "Eventually he started calling too. Then it all abruptly ended a little after two in the morning."

"I'm sorry," Bethany said.

"Don't worry about it. I tried calling you after his first message, but when he made a nuisance out of himself, I put my phone on vibrate."

'Two. Maybe that's when the effect stopped? Six hours after I take it? Or is it 4 hours after the guy is around me? Ugh. I should've asked.'

"Well," Tiff said. "Let's try it again."

"What?"

"I've got nothing better to do today. Besides, I owe you a birthday anyway," Tiff said with a wink. "Drink up, and we'll go to the farmer's market."

Bethany's eyes widened. "You're kidding right?"

Tiff pushed the bottle to her. "Not in the least. Let's go."

In record time, Bethany was back in the kitchen, dressed and ready to go. She exhaled deeply staring at the bottle.

"Nasty?" Tiff asked.

"You have no idea."

She got everything ready on the counter including several slices of bread to eat after she drank it.

"Gonna take a whole spoonful again?"

Bethany shrugged. "I know that amount works." She lifted the spoon to her mouth then hesitated. "You should know this stuff turns the eye of women too." It might not be the best idea to take it around her friend.

"That's fine. I'm not into women."

"I don't think that matters," Bethany giggled.

"Well, fine. I apologize in advance for any moves I might make on you. How about that?"

Bethany rolled her eyes. She pinched her nose with one hand and swallowed the rot reeking sludge. As soon as it was down, she began eating the bread. They waited until her stomach settled before they left. Tiff never did show any indication she was attracted to her. If the potion affected her, she hid it well.

They walked along Main Street where the market was set up, browsing through fresh produce and handmade soaps. Tiff was in a constant state of shock at the crowd forming behind Bethany. Many men were following her around, a few with girlfriends who were vocalizing their objections. They had to leave before they caused a scene.

Bethany picked out several white peaches and was about to pay when a handsome man named Levi stepped up to treat her. "Allow me," he said, opening his wallet.

"I'll see you later," Tiff said, maneuvering her way out of the crowd.

Bethany barely paid attention to her, but got the text later which read, "Where was this shit when I was single?"

Levi put his arm around her waist and walked her to his car. It took two minutes to get there, and he was already on the verge of taking her in the parking lot in front of everyone. "Where are we going?" he asked breathlessly.

"Your place," she said, thinking it was better he not learn where she lived. She was already worried about Mark showing up at some point.

"Uh," he said, opening the door for her. "I've got a couple of roommates." He closed the door and walked to the other side.

'Roommates? I've always wanted to experience more than one cock at a time.'

"Would they be game?" she asked when he got behind the wheel.

He looked at her shocked. "With a beautiful woman like you? Are you sure?"

Bethany nodded.

"Damn, I'm glad I met you," he grinned. He pulled out of the lot and drove to the three bedroom duplex he shared with two other guys near the college campus.

Once inside his home, he ran through, pounding on doors, yelling at his buddies to wake up. "I've got a surprise for you!"

They came out of their rooms, half awake, and cussing him for interrupting their sleep until they saw her. It didn't take more than a few seconds for their lust to brew. Then it was every man for themselves as they tried to be the one closest to her. Levi let them know she wanted to take them all, and the clothes started flying while Bethany laughed. *'This can't be real.'*

It had been far too long since she had a good fucking, and now she had three hot strapping college guys tripping over themselves to get to her first. *'Why not?'* She kept telling herself.

'No one has to ever know.'

They swarmed her with compliments, and they approached and retreated like they expected her to change her mind at any moment. She kissed each of the three young men in turn and felt their cock while she did. They were all impressive in their own way. All of them yanked themselves hard when she was paying attention to someone else. She was barely in the door of the duplex and felt sorely overdressed.

"Where do you want me?" she asked.

"Here," one of the boys said. He grabbed her hand and led her down the hall to his bedroom. "Mine's the biggest."

Bethany giggled over what he said even though she knew he was talking about the bed. It was a queen, so it was still going to be crowded. But, it was much better than the futon she pictured.

"Me first," Levi shouted. "I brought her."

It should upset her being treated like something he bought at the market, but it didn't. She was enjoying the flattery from all of them anxious to have her.

Levi put his arms around her and pulled her to him, kissing her hard on the mouth. Her lips parted, and Levi's tongue darted into her hungry mouth. He soon removed her jacket and tossed it across the room. His hands roughly squeezed her breasts. It might have been just his inexperience causing him to be so callous, but she loved it.

Her nipples hardened, and she felt her panties moisten with her warm juices. She ran her hands across his bare chest. He was very muscular with six pack abs. The other guys might be able to give him a run for his money in the athletic department, but he was the fittest man she'd ever seen naked.

He took a step backward and ripped open her blouse.

Buttons flew everywhere. He pulled her bra down, exposing her breasts. Holding them in his hands, his tongue found one hard nipple while he squeezed the other with two fingers. Bethany moaned out her approval.

Another guy stepped up to her side. "What's your name?" she asked. His messy blonde hair fell in waves over his face.

"Jordan," he answered. He lowered his head and kissed her neck.

There was a set of hands on her back which ran down and cupped her ass through her jeans. "These have to go," a voice said.

Before Bethany could move, the hands wrapped around her and unfastened her jeans. He shimmied them and her panties down her legs to the floor where she kicked out of them and her ballet slippers. The same set of hands unclasped her bra, and she pulled her arms through it.

Finally, he walked around to her other side. "Wes," he grinned. He then playfully shoved Levi out of the way and took over caressing her breasts.

"Hey!" Levi shouted.

"There's enough to go around," Bethany reassured them.

Jordan shook his head and slapped Levi on the back. "Damn, dude! We owe you big!"

Bethany motioned them away from her, and they all retreated with forlorn looks on their faces like they had been rejected. She climbed onto the edge of the bed, and asked, "How are we going to do this? Who's first?"

They practically fell over each other clambering to join her.

"Me!" Levi said again, claiming his right to dibs since he was the one who met her originally.

She pulled Levi to her and kissed him before spinning onto

her stomach with her legs on the floor. Her ass was lifted high in the air, inviting him. "There's room for more," she said. She outstretched her arms and patted the bed in front of her.

Jordan reached her first, shoving his cock in her face. It was at least seven inches long and thick. She took it as deep into her mouth as she could. He grabbed her hair and roughly fucked into her face.

Behind her, Levi spread her ass cheeks and dropped to the floor, licking at her already wet pussy from below. Her first orgasm was already building.

There was a frustrated sigh, and she reached her hand out in the direction it came from, motioning for Wes to come closer. When she felt him nearby, she grabbed his shaft and began stroking it.

Levi positioned himself and placed the tip of his cock at her entrance. He leaned forward, and slid into her well lubricated tunnel. Bethany thrust back to meet him, swallowing every inch of his member with her pussy. He fucked her hard, with no rhythm, his little experience showing, but she still climaxed quickly. The arousal from having three men surround her alone could bring her to orgasm. Her moans were muffled by Jordan's huge cock in her mouth.

"Where do you want me to cum?" Levi's voice was a breathless whisper.

Bethany pushed against Jordan's hips to move him away. "In my mouth," she said.

"Switch!" Wes yelled.

The three of them rotated around her. Wes was behind her now, slamming his six inch shaft into her, balls deep.

Levi barely got his tip in her mouth before he began bucking and shuddering, shooting his load down her throat. When it was over, he laid back on the bed, pouting. No doubt he was upset for not outlasting his buddies.

"Let's try something," Jordan suggested. He told Wes to back off a minute.

"No," Wes insisted.

It took some effort for Jordan to convince him to change positions, but eventually both guys backed away from her. There had been some hushed voices in their conversation, but Bethany heard every word.

Jordan lay on his back and grabbed Bethany, pulling her over top of him. His cock was by far the largest and would stretch her wide. She carefully climbed over him and lowered herself onto his shaft. She couldn't take more than an inch or two before having to lift up and try again. Each time she came down on him, a little more of his cock slipped inside her until finally she had his full length buried deep into her.

"Oh my god!" she practically screamed. Her orgasm began halfway down his shaft and wasn't ending. The only sensation she felt was her pussy crammed with cock, barely able to hold it all.

The grin on his face proved this wasn't the first time a woman couldn't take him all before cumming. He guided her with his hands. Slowly she fucked him while her moans were constantly screaming forth. "Damn," she muttered over and over.

Wes' hands pushed on her back, forcing her down onto Jordan. Her breasts smashed against his chiseled chest. Wes crouched over top of both of them, and the tip of his cock pressed against her tight ass hole.

He plunged forward with force and broke his way through.

He pulled out and drove into her again. Then again until her ass was filled with his cock.

"Oh, yes! That's it, boys! Fuck me good!"

Levi found his second wind, and she felt him slap her face gently with his now hard cock to get her attention. She opened her mouth and turned toward him, letting him fuck her face.

Jordan came first. His massive cock swelled larger than she thought possible before he exploded inside her. Wes was right after him, cumming deep in her ass.

Bethany was spent. She allowed Levi's cock to fall from her mouth, and she half assed jacked him while catching her breath. She was too exhausted for much more. He took over, finishing the job himself and aiming for her open mouth when he shot his load.

The four of them collapsed on the bed for several minutes. One by one, the three guys began to perk up. Their hands traveled her body again. When one hand reached her clit, Bethany pulled herself upright and turned away.

"No more?" Jordan asked.

"Maybe after a bit of clean up and a power nap," she suggested.

The three men moaned, but ultimately agreed. Jordan went straight to sleep on his bed while Bethany found her scattered clothing and got dressed. She tied the shirt together over her bra and covered herself up with the jacket. All that was left were the shoes which she slipped on. The other two ransacked the kitchen for something to eat.

When she came out to join them, their faces dropped. "Are you leaving?" Levi asked.

"I thought there was going to be a round two," Wes said.

"There will be," Bethany lied. "I'm going to grab a bite too if that's okay?"

"Of course," Levi said. He pushed the box of crackers across to her.

Bethany smiled and pulled one out of the box. "Then I'm just gonna freshen up a bit before joining you in the bedroom again."

Wes walked out of the kitchen saying, "It's the second door on the right," as he went.

She wanted to sneak out, but Levi wasn't leaving her alone. He hung around waiting for her. It's like he could read her mind.

Bethany hadn't paid attention to the time all morning. She wasn't sure how much longer she had until the potion wore off. There was definitely enough time for a round two, but she didn't want to risk falling asleep afterward. *'I don't want to find out what would happen if I'm still here then.'*

"Alright," she announced after eating a handful of stale crackers.

Levi motioned for her to go first. She stopped at the bathroom, and Levi stopped too. "I'll be right in," she told him, nodding at the bedroom where they all just fucked.

Inside the bathroom, she text Tiff, asking where she was. Luckily, Tiff hadn't gone home yet. She had just left a coffee shop wondering if she still needed to stick around just in case.

"Do you know that Italian place on the corner of Ash?" Bethany asked. It was around the corner and at the end of the block. She remembered passing it on the way.

"Yeah," Tiff replied. "Great breadsticks."

"Meet me there." Bethany peeked out into the hallway, and it was empty. "NOW!" she sent.

Jordan's bedroom was farther down the hallway. If she had to walk past it, she'd be screwed. Literally. She opened the door just enough to sneak through it. She locked the bathroom door behind her. This way they might think she was still in there long enough for her to meet up with Tiff. If any of them came after her, she wouldn't be able to out run them.

She tip toed through the living room and let herself out. The walk to the restaurant was short, and she glanced over her shoulder the entire way. Tiff was already waiting, parked along the street.

Tiff took one look at her and shook her head. "I love Brad dearly, but if I ever find myself single again, you've got to hook me up with that nasty ass potion!"

The two of them laughed as Tiff drove off with Bethany spilling all of the details of her latest slutty exploit.

Chapter Four

Sunday

"I've been looking for you my whole life," Adam whispered in her ear.

The words sounded wonderful, but it was just the potion talking. Bethany was wise to remember that.

He laid her carefully onto the sand and kissed her passionately. There was something a little different about him than the other experiences she'd had with the love potion. He was more delicate, loving in the way he touched her. Mark and the college guys had been eager to consume her, but Adam was taking his time.

Bethany needed to get to bed early that night because the work week started in the morning. It was always harder for her to fall asleep on Sunday nights even if the weekend had been boring and uneventful. That's why she took to the beach this afternoon, love potion in hand.

The temperature wasn't too bad, but it was overcast and windy. There were far fewer options here than she'd hoped. Most of the men she saw were walking hand in hand with someone, and she didn't want to be a homewrecker. Chrissy aside, she wasn't out to break up relationships.

Then she saw him. Adam jogged right past her, and he was gorgeous. He was alone, but that didn't mean he was single. He stopped about twenty yards down the shore and began to stretch. It was more secluded down this way. The beach ended not far past him where the rock structures protruded out into the water.

'*It's perfect.*' Bethany pulled the bottle from her pocket, poured some potion into the plastic spoon she brought with her. She wasn't expecting to do much today, so she didn't want to take it until she was sure she needed it. Then from her other pocket, she removed a sandwich baggie containing three slices of bread. It took barely a minute for her to down the potion and start cramming bread into her mouth. Everything went back into her pockets and she chugged a bottle of water before popping a couple breath mints. She was rather proud of herself when she was done.

The jogger was only a few feet ahead of her now. He stopped stretching and turned to face her.

'*This could never get old,*' she thought. Bethany spun around and began walking away from him. In a few seconds, he had run up and came around in front of her, cutting her off.

"What's your name?" he asked. "I come here every weekend, but I've never seen you."

"Bethany," she said, shyly glancing at her feet. There was something in his gaze. There was lust, desire, but there was something else she didn't recognize. She'd never been looked at in that way until now. She liked it, but didn't know how to respond.

"I'm Adam," he told her with a smile that melted her.

They walked together back in the direction he had been jogging. The way the water, sand and rock had all cut there grooves into the area made one little spot secluded from the rest of the beach. Anyone could walk out this way, but for right now it was just the two of them, staring out at the ocean.

That's where they sat to talk. Adam pulled a blanket out of his bag and put it out on the sand for them to sit. It was like they were old friends who had ran into each other. Old friends with intimate knowledge of each other. They kissed. Their hands roamed each other's bodies. But, they talked for a couple hours. One thing led to another, and they were making out.

Bethany was laying on her back with one leg out of her leggings. This massive hunk of a man was over top of her, excitedly lapping at her clit. The fear of being caught was exhilarating. It turned her on immensely, but it was also preventing her from fully enjoying Adam. She wasn't able to cum even though Adam was extraordinarily skilled.

"Do you enjoy what I'm doing?" Adam asked concerned.

"Yeah," she said, propping up on her elbows. "I'm just afraid of someone walking up on us."

Adam sat next to her, staring at the water again.

"No, don't stop," she insisted. "It'll be fine."

He smiled at her and pulled his shorts down over his running shoes. He knelt between her legs and leaned down on top of her. "Is this okay? Or would you rather be on top to keep an eye out?"

They laughed. "No, I'd rather not see anyone coming."

Bethany barely peeked at Adam's cock. It was large. She could tell that by the bulge in his shorts. She was not expecting the vastness of his size until he was burying his shaft inside of her. Jordan had been well endowed, but Adam made him seem small.

She kept her moans low and quiet, biting her lower lip to help mute herself until she could taste her own blood. Adam kept pummeling into her. One orgasm after another with the sound of the waves crashing onto the beach behind them. The chilliness of the afternoon gave way to two sweat soaked bodies unable to get enough of each other.

Her body climaxed too many times to count. Adam shifted positions a few times. He lowered himself close to her chest then straightened his arms to lift off her. He pulled her legs over his shoulder and moved them both to one side. The one thing he never did was stop.

He was elevated over her and put all his weight on one arm. With his other hand, he rubbed her clit.

"Oh fuck!" Bethany moaned.

"Like that?"

"Mmm-hmm."

"Say it," he demanded.

"I like that," she said.

Yet again, her juices flowed out of her and down his shaft. He thrust into her hard and slow until her orgasm subsided then began fucking her hard and fast again.

"Oh, my god! Not so soon," she pleaded.

"Why not?"

"Because it's ... driving me ... insane," she said in ragged breaths.

"Good," Adam said. He arched her legs over his shoulders and plowed her pussy with his cock while her moans rose to high pitched squeals.

"Ready?" he asked after her next climax.

"For what?"

He didn't answer right away, but he finally told her he was getting close. As soon as the words were out of his mouth, he began to buck and twitch. Right before he came, he pulled out and shot into the sand next to the blanket.

Bethany rolled to her side. She knew they'd been fucking for quite a while, but was surprised to see how dark it had become.

Adam collapsed next to her and held her. She could've stayed in his arms all night. Eventually her body cooled off, and she got a shiver.

"We should get dressed and get going before we freeze," he said, sitting up.

They found their clothes, and Adam grabbed all his gear. They walked along the beach together in silence. Bethany worried about what he was thinking, if the potion was still as potent as when she took it, or if it was starting to wear off. Then he grabbed her hand and held it until they reached the top of the stairs and had made it to the parking lot.

"Can I see you again?" he asked.

Bethany nodded. "Sure."

He grabbed a piece of scrap paper from his car and wrote his number on it, handing it to her. After a long kiss goodbye, he drove off.

She slipped the paper in her jacket pocket. She was tempted to call him. Seeing him again wasn't off the table for her, but it wouldn't be the same without the potion. She wasn't going to buy it and use it daily for an entire relationship either.

Bethany got in her car and drove to her building. It was far later than she had planned on being out. In fact, this was exactly why she went to the beach in the early afternoon instead of going out on the town in the evening. She had an early start the next day, and now, she was going to be ass dragging at work.

'Worth it,' she thought.

Chapter Five

Monday

Bethany left work and didn't dread going home for the first time since her break up. Work was the one place where she had human interaction. As stressful as her job could be at times, she enjoyed talking with others and being connected to them.

Everything she needed was with her in an old lunchbox in her car. As she was getting it ready to drink the potion, she was laughing, thinking anyone halfway paying attention to her might believe she was readying her drugs. Instead it was a gross sludge which was worth every disgusting drop. This time she poured the spoonful over a slice of bread and folded it up. Using both hands, she shoved it into her mouth then hit both hands on the steering wheel as she tried to chew it up quickly. Small droplets leaked from her eyes as she tried to control her breaths with a mouth full of bread to avoid puking. This would be the last time she tried it this way.

Once it was swallowed, and she was sure it was going to stay down, she checked her makeup in the mirror. The outfit she was wearing was borderline between office attire and going out. It made her look a little boring to wear it to a bar, and on a normal day, she'd go home and completely change. There was no need tonight, not with the potion on her side. She glanced around the parking lot making sure there were no stragglers. She slid off her hose and panties then removed her bra without taking off her

"

dress. The cute scarf which had been wrapped around her neck most of the day was now hung over the front of the dress thinly covering her perky breasts, and her nipples which stood out and poked through the fabric.

She chose the bar simply because it was close to home. When she walked in the door, she secretly looked around, taking note of who was available. There were a few guys playing pool, a couple at the counter, and four men at the dartboards. Two of the latter had girlfriends with them. She took a seat at the bar. By the time she sat down and looked up again, she had three men surrounding her.

It was the first time she had the luxury of choosing like this. Based on appearances alone, she picked the one most attractive to her. He was a tall, beefy man with a five o'clock shadow. His hands were rough like he worked construction or some other manual job. She smiled at him, and he bought her a drink.

The other two men looked disappointed and took a step away. They didn't leave. They stuck around in case the first one struck out.

The man introduced himself as Danny and bought her a drink. After a couple sips, she took a large swig for courage. "Would you like to get out of here?" she asked.

He took her hand and led her out of the bar toward his truck across the parking lot. Bethany stopped and tugged at him, nodding for them to head another way. They walked down the alley along the side of the bar.

"What are you doing?" Danny asked.

"I can't wait," she said, grabbing him by the shoulders. She had to stand on her tip toes to reach him, and even then, it was with difficulty. She pulled him to her and kissed him hard.

The street light nearby blinked quickly on and off before going out for good as if it understood their need for privacy. A slight breeze hit them, and she felt the way it blew her hair aside, exposing her neck. Danny noticed too because it was the first place he brought his mouth to explore.

Either her directness or the exposing of her neck, or both, was enough to do in Danny. She could feel the hardness under his jeans rubbing against her when he leaned in close.

While he kissed and nibbled from one ear to the other, she brought one had across her breasts. She teased both nipples and allowed a small moan to escape her lips. The sound brought his attention back to her. He stared into her eyes with pure lust for only a moment before crushing her lips with his.

When he pulled back, they were both breathless and flushed. He brushed his calloused thumb over her lower lip, and asked, "Are you sure? Here?"

"Haven't you ever done anything crazy?" Bethany bit her lip and gave him a playful look.

He searched her eyes for something then lowered his head to her breasts. He teased her nipples with his teeth through the fabric. His hands roamed down her sides until they found the bottom of her dress and inched it up. Once he discovered how naked she was underneath, it was his turn to moan. "For fucks sake," he cried out. "Where did you come from?"

Bethany giggled and reached for the button at the top of his jeans. It was ready to pop from the material being expanded from the size of his hard cock. She pulled down the zipper and freed his member. It was massive and took both hands for her to work it with any skill.

Danny positioned his hip against her, holding her dress

hiked far enough up for access while freeing his hands. He massaged her breasts, bringing his mouth first to one, then the other.

She was almost exposed from the waist down, but his thick build blocked her from view not that there was anyone around to watch. His stiff cock was throbbing in her hands. She carefully supported it with one hand while trying to pull his ass hugging jeans down with the other. After struggling for a minute, he helped her and slid them down just past his ass.

He ran his hands up her back and back down to her thighs as he pulled her closer. He pulled back and opened his mouth to speak.

"No talking," Bethany said, pressing her lips on his again and exploring his mouth with her tongue. Men had never flocked to her before, and this was the wildest thing she'd ever done. Her pussy was rocked with excitement, and she needed his shaft filling her soon. There was no time for unnecessary chit chat. This was going to happen.

He grabbed her hips with both hands and picked her off the ground. She wrapped her legs around him and could barely hook her ankles together behind his back. His cock throbbed between her legs, and she could almost cum from the sensation extending up to her clit.

She wrapped her arms around his neck to help him balance her against the brick wall of the side of the bar. He leaned forward and bit the flesh of her exposed neck once again. Then he pulled back just enough for the tip of his member to catch in the opening of her tunnel before driving it forward as deep as he could.

It was only a couple inches, but his girth was staggering.

Bethany would've let out a small scream of excitement if his mouth hadn't quieted her with a kiss. He pulled back and entered again, drilling a little deeper the second time. Over and over, he entered her deeper until finally his full length had penetrated her.

Her legs kept slipping off him, and she brought them back up until finally she gave up. One leg dangled at their side while he held the other against him at an angle. She held on around his shoulders and felt her dress catching on the rough brick behind her. It would leave a mess of scratches down her back, but she barely noticed the pain in the moment.

Every thrust spread her wider, and she couldn't believe she accommodate all of him. His was the largest cock she'd ever seen, let alone felt ripping her open to own her pussy.

His mouth found its way back to her neck once she became too exhausted to scream. Each driving force into her box was met with a nibble. The bites became harder the closer to orgasm he came.

Bethany's labyrinth convulsed around him as she came over and over. It was hard to tell where one orgasm ended and the next began. She squeezed her inner muscles around him as tight as she could, and her eyes rolled back in her head. She felt close to passing out when she felt his cock throbbing inside her and realized he was close.

"Oh, fuck," he mumbled, shooting his load deep into her. The warm sensation coated her tunnel.

When he was finished, he lowered her leg and helped her find balance on her feet again. Her legs were weak and could barely hold her upright, but she faked it the best she could.

"What do we do now?" he asked.

Bethany looked up at him confused. She leaned against the wall for support. If he thought there was a round two in the near future, he was wrong. It would be all she manage just to get home after this.

"Do you want to go somewhere? Or maybe head back inside for a drink?"

Her throat was dry making it difficult to form the first few words. "I.. am... thirsty," she said. "A drink sounds good."

Danny smiled at her and wrapped his arm around her waist, walking her out of the alley toward the parking lot at the front of the bar. She pulled away from him before they reached the door. He stopped and grabbed onto her.

"I just want to check myself in the car first," she told him. "You know, don't want to make a scene when we go back inside," she chuckled nervously.

"Gotcha," Danny winked. "Which one is yours?"

"There," she pointed to her car.

He started to walk her to it.

"I'll only be a minute," she said, giving him the hint to leave her.

Danny leaned down and kissed her again. It was gentler this time, but still filled with passion. Then he said, "See you in a minute," before heading to the door.

She walked the last several feet to her car on shaky legs, but she made it and fell into the driver's seat. One look in the mirror showed a guilty face with smeared and shiny makeup. She turned the car on, but powdered her nose while keeping an eye out in case he came back.

Then she threw it in reverse and practically peeled out of the parking lot to leave. She sped down the street like a criminal and ran a red light, afraid he might follow her somehow. Taking a long zig-zagging route and three times as long to get home as it should, she was finally convinced he wasn't looking for her. The sex was amazing, but someone like him didn't usually find someone like her attractive. She couldn't afford to buy enough of the potion for a full relationship. The last thing she wanted was to be around when it wore off.

At her apartment, she noticed a couple gawkers on the street. Her legs weren't up to making a quick run inside. She kept her fingers wrapped around the pepper spray in her purse and walked straight to the building door without looking at any of the men who stopped as they were walking past. Once in her apartment, she felt silly for being so afraid. None of them so much as whistled. If she had talked to them, she was sure she'd be in a good position for dessert, but she was still full from the buffet Danny served.

Bethany took a long hot shower and thought about what to do next. She was looking for love after all. These random encounters were amazing, but she should use the potion as an ice breaker to find someone who would want to stick around long term.

She wrapped her hair in a towel and put on her robe. Taking her laptop to bed with her, she logged back into the dating sites she hadn't used in ages, updating her profiles. They had never worked for her before, but it didn't hurt to try again.

Chapter Six

Tuesday

The dating profiles she updated were hot with activity when she woke up that morning. It really came as no surprise. Bethany wasn't a conceited person, but she was far from ugly. The hardest part about dating sites was weeding out the guys who still lived in their parents' basements, who had no jobs or license, or who were only interested in sex.

None of that mattered today. All she had to do was find the most attractive man who sent a message, but even that was proving to be a hard task. Many were neck and neck in the looks category.

Shortly after getting logged into her computer at work, she settled on Bruce. There wasn't really anything to set him apart from the rest. She chose him based on his name only. Bruce sounded like a manly man. He sounded like the type of guy who knew how to fuck hard and dirty. She could only hope she was right.

Most of the people on these sites didn't pay for a membership. They counted on the other person shelling out the dough to enable them to send a message, or they gave out their phone numbers right away. That was something Bethany normally didn't do, but she could, and definitely would, block him once she got what she wanted.

She replied to his brief introductory message telling him a

few things about herself. She began each line with a digit. If he read them down, he'd have her phone number, and she prayed he was smart enough to figure it out. Sometimes prayers are answered.

By lunch, she had barely gotten any work done. They'd been texting each other nonstop. It took all of her attention to keep the conversation going when most of his replies accumulated to, "K," or, "Yeah."

'And men actually wonder why they get ghosted. If you want to get to know someone, and keep their interest, you have to do more than that.'

At any other time, she'd have given up before her first coffee break. It was too much effort. She wasn't trying to find romance tonight. All she wanted was new dick to test drive. The pictures she asked him to send looked very promising. Whenever she heard footsteps nearby, she'd place her phone face down on her desk and let her fingers fly over the keyboard. Otherwise, she was being paid to convince Bruce to meet her tonight.

Most men couldn't wait to dive in without testing the waters. She had to pick the one and, quite possibly, only single man on the planet who didn't want to meet right away. Bethany had to lay it on thick with a made up schedule stating she'd be unavailable after tonight for up to two weeks.

"It makes sense," she told him. "Meet now. See if there's a spark."

Bruce finally agreed to meet her at a bookshop. His mom's birthday was coming up, so he could pick her up a gift card while he was there. The two of them would get something at the coffee shop in the back of the store and chat in person for a while. Nothing too serious.

Those words caused a huge grin to plaster Bethany's face, and she had a hard time ridding herself of it the rest of the day. She wasn't sure if Bruce wasn't the type of guy to jump in bed with someone, or if he just wanted her to believe that. It was probably the latter. Either way, she could almost guarantee the night would end in sex.

They had agreed to meet in the coffee shop. Well, not exactly agreed. Bethany suggested they meet out front, but Bruce thought meeting inside was better. She never told him she'd do it, but knew that was what he was expecting. It worried her to walk through the store after drinking the potion. There could be any number of guys inside, and Bruce might not be able to keep his hands to himself whether they were in a public place or not.

She arrived about fifteen minutes early and swallowed a spoonful of nasty from the decorative bottle. The piece of bread she shoved in her mouth afterward did little to help. It had worked the first couple of times, but it wasn't cutting it anymore. The only thing she had with her was a bottle of water which wouldn't do anything to cover the taste. She popped a handful of mints into her mouth and chewed them while her tongue felt like it was on fire from the spicy spearmint flavor.

Bethany walked up to the front of the building and waited on the sidewalk near the doors. She glanced around nervously, not sure what to do if another man approached before Bruce. She was beginning to embrace her newfound sluttiness. If the man looked good enough to eat and was alone, she might go ahead and leave with him, standing up Bruce in the process.

It didn't come to that. Bruce approached about a minute later. "I thought that was you. Decide not to meet inside?" He asked from several feet away.

She watched the look in his eyes change as he got closer. It went from friendly, to curiously confused, to strictly lust in seconds. When he reached her, he kept walking forward a few more steps, backing her off the walkway, through the shrubbery, and against the wall of the store.

"My," he moaned softly. "You're the most intoxicating woman I've ever met."

Bethany giggled and lifted her chin up to receive the kiss she knew was coming. It started slow which surprised her, but he must've run out of restraint quickly. After a couple seconds, he pressed his mouth onto hers harder, grabbing her hips in the process. It was hard to wiggle free because there was no room behind her to move away, but when she finally did, she breathlessly whispered, "Want to go somewhere?"

He grabbed her hand and led her back to his truck. The parking area on this end of the strip mall had a dozen or so cars when they arrived. Anyone outside was walking to and from the shops, not paying attention to the couple acting like horny teenagers in the cab, at least not yet.

Bruce turned the key in the ignition, but that was the farthest they got. He reached over and grabbed her leg, pulling her closer to him on the bench seat. With his mouth covering hers, his hands roamed her breasts, squeezing and caressing them in succession. One hand quickly traveled down and rubbed her over her jeans, making her ready now. She went from being afraid someone may wander down the beach and catch her to not caring if the entire parking lot gathered round for a free show within days. The potion was certainly breaking down her walls if nothing else.

Bruce's cock was rock hard and strained against the denim

material of his jeans. She could feel how tight it was when she ran her hand across blindly. She fumbled with the button and zipper until she had it freed and in her hands.

He grabbed the lower part of her shirt and lifted it over her head, keeping her arms trapped in the sleeves. Effortlessly, he unsnapped her bra with one hand and let it hang loose while he teased her nipples with his teeth. One hand kept ahold of her shirt behind her head while the other hand worked on removing her jeans.

'It's not the first time he's had someone in the cab of his truck.' Bethany would've giggled, but he had briefly brought his mouth back to her lips, and his tongue was exploring hers. The last time she'd had sex in a car was in high school, and even that was rare. Bruce was in complete control of the situation and moved with confident experience. *'I bet he had a truck then too,'* she thought.

Once he had her pants off, he laid her back on the bench seat. He kissed her again, and she melted into it. Her arms were still trapped, but he no longer held the shirt in place. If she wanted to, she could wiggle her way free, but she didn't try.

One of his hands pulled down his jeans while the other rubbed her clit. Bethany had thought she was hot and on fire before, but now she could feel her pussy throbbing, aching for release. Bruce worked his hand against her swollen outer lips, and she raised her hips off the seat, encouraging him. The thought of possibly being caught worked its way back into her mind, and the idea turned her on even more.

He grabbed her around the waist and pulled her in tight. His mouth explored her breasts once again. He took one hard nipple into his mouth then the other. Back and forth, he suckled, licked and nibbled the hard nubs. Her body shivered as electric shocks shot from her tits, down her torso, and directly to her clit. It felt so good her legs began to quiver like an orgasm was erupting within her.

The hand he slid around her waist worked its way down her ass. He groped her cheeks as his mouth wandered down her chest to her abdomen then lower yet. He was now pressed bare assed against the window of the truck, and Bethany was thankful it was dark. A sight like that would be hard to miss in the daytime, and she hoped the shoppers would be too lost in their own thoughts to pay attention to anything happening around them. Bruce flicked the tip of his tongue over her clit, just enough to tease.

Bethany bucked up against him when he did, but he lifted himself away quickly. He brought his body down over hers and said, "No time for that now." He nodded toward the windshield. "We could be caught at any moment. Unfortunately for both of us, we can't linger out here too long."

He nudged her leg over until it was bent with her foot on the floorboard. He positioned himself between her legs and touched the head of his shaft to her opening. He braced himself with his hands on the back and edge of the seat then pushed forward. He slowly pumped in and out of her aching pussy.

She was happy to finally be full of his swollen cock. The thoughts of an audience had been pushed completely from her mind.

Bruce tasted her nipple again then brought his lips to hers. He urgently kissed her as he increased the pace of his fucking until he was ramming her so hard, her arms began to hit against the passenger door. It's what caused her to finally free herself from the shirt trap that helped hold her body in place.

She raised her hips to meet each thrust. They were two insatiable lovers, fucking each other as hard as they could. Her labyrinth began to convulse around his cock as an orgasm rocked through her. He began grunting and twitching. He was almost there, and she bit her lower lip until she tasted blood, riding out her climax while his shaft engorged inside her just before his release. Her hot juices gushed, coating his shaft and balls. Her tunnel continuously contracted over his member until his explosion was complete.

They lay there gasping for air for several minutes after it was over, completely oblivious to remembering where they were. Finally, Bruce lifted himself off her and peeked around. "Looks like the coast is clear."

Bethany sat up slowly and redressed. This was the hard part. It was the one thing she couldn't completely plan ahead of time: the getaway.

"I wonder if anyone saw and went inside, or went to their car to report it."

She squinted her eyes in the darkness, but couldn't see anyone sitting in the vehicle.

"I still have to get that gift card too."

Bethany nodded. "You should do that."

"You coming?" he asked.

"No, I'll go to my car and wait for you. Just in case," she smiled at him. "If I see a cop car, I'll text you a head's up."

The two of them laughed.

"Actually, that's not a bad idea. Where you parked?"

"Two rows over," she said, pointing out the windshield.

"Alright. See you in a few." Bruce gave her a quick kiss then hopped out of the truck with Bethany right behind him.

As soon as he walked through the door of the bookshop, she put her car in reverse. His number was blocked before she made it out of the parking lot. Her heart raced like she had just done something illegal, which she had, but that wasn't what caused her to be flustered. It was dipping out on a guy for the second time in as many days which had her worked up.

Chapter Seven

Wednesday

Most of the office was dreading the party tonight. Their boss went out of his way to make it the most unbearable event every year. He had gotten better. It used to be held right before Christmas which put a strain on all the employees as they were trying to get their last minute holiday preparations and shopping done. As the years went by, the attendance kept dwindling.

It still wasn't mandatory to attend, but if Mr. Greene could figure out a legal way to make it so, he would have done it already. Instead, he held their Christmas bonus as a short term ransom. They had two choices. They could come to the party and get their bonus check randomly throughout the night. It was ill advised to ask him for it directly. He'd see to it yours was the last to be distributed if that happened. Brown nosing was out too. Those who kissed ass to him, buttered him up, hovered around him, hoping he'd dole out their check were forced to wait longer. It was a game of chance. Show up, participate, act like it was a fun time, and eventually, Mr. Greene would offer the ticket to leave: the bonus check.

It was always held the Wednesday night before the holiday weekend. The timing still posed problems for those hosting dinner the next day or traveling out of town. Still, it was a choice. If waiting until the payday before Christmas for the bonus wasn't a problem, skip the party.

This year's theme was a masquerade ball. The entire office groaned last year with the 80's retro party because it had been so overdone. That was nothing compared to the dislike for the masquerade.

Bethany had been dreading it since it was announced in mid-October. The only thing causing her to change her mind was Billy. Well, two things: Billy and the love potion. He was bad news. All of the hot men typically were. She and all the other ladies working there had lusted after him since he was hired two years ago. Even the married women secretly fantasized about him, picturing Billy in their minds when they gave it up to their husband's at home.

He was one of those guys who was well aware of how good he looked. He knew he could get any woman he wanted, and he used it to his advantage. Women like Bethany weren't given the time of day by him. Others he treated like his own personal assistants who he kept on delicate strings. They did his bidding in the hopes he'd flash one of his smiles bearing the dimple on his left cheek. They really hoped for far more than that, but all they ever got were some flirtation and if they were lucky, unfulfilled promises.

Tonight was her chance. Everyone had to wear a mask which meant he might not recognize her right off the bat. Even if he did, the potion would do the heavy lifting for her. Once the idea hit her, she couldn't wipe the smile off her face. *I'm going to fuck the hell out of Billy tonight,'* she kept thinking.

When she dressed for the party, she took every preparation she could think of into consideration. The gown she wore was long and wouldn't be easy to get back on herself, so she didn't wear anything under it. Billy could easily lift the material over her ass and take her from behind. She also pulled her hair up in an elegant do. She always wore it down or at most, in a ponytail. This would make it harder to recognize her even without the mask. There were over two hundred people employed in her building, and she wanted to make sure Billy couldn't figure out she was the one who worked across the same floor as he did who was always trying to make small talk with him unsuccessfully.

The dress came with a matching clutch, and she had to search her room for almost an hour to find it. She had never planned on using it, but she needed a safe place to stash the potion. Instead of bread, she was just going to wash it down with a glass of punch.

Once she was at the party, she waited and hoped he showed. He didn't always come to them, but she had overheard him telling someone he could really use the money sooner than later. The evening was growing old, and she was about to give up when he finally made an entrance. Even with the disguises, he was easy to spot. Between his muscled jaw and that trademark dimple, there was only one Billy.

She walked up behind him and took a big sip straight from the bottle with one hand then gulped down the punch she was holding in the other. The empty glass she sat on the nearest table, and called out to him in a sing song voice about an octave higher than her normal tone while stashing the potion back in her handbag. "Hi, Billy," she crooned.

He turned around straight away. She couldn't judge his initial reaction with half his face covered, but she watched the rest of his body relax. The potion hadn't let her down, not that she expected it would.

"Come with me," she sang out, holding out her hand.

She led him to the hallway. Once they were out of sight, she pulled him close. He needed no further encouragement. His hand was already dipping into the neckline of her dress, groping at her breasts. "You're the most beautiful woman I've ever seen," he said.

Bethany hoped her eye mask blocked him from seeing her eyes roll. *'He sees me every single day, and I am positive he has never thought twice about me.'*

"Where should we go?" she asked. They couldn't stay in the open hallway. Someone would venture this way eventually. They wouldn't be the first couple caught in the act, but she didn't want to face the rumor mill at work. Plus, Billy would be rather disappointed to learn who he was actually with tonight.

He looked around then smiled. "I know the perfect place!" He grabbed her hand and led her to the elevator, pressing the call button repeatedly as if it was going to make the doors open any faster.

Once the doors shut behind them, he pressed a floor button and pushed her into the corner. He was all over her. His mouth couldn't make up its mind between her lips, ears and neck. His hands wandered up and down her body from her breasts, to her ass, and back. She convinced herself it was the potion making him so clumsy with the moves. He couldn't be bad in bed normally. Any man who looked that good had to have enough experience to be a skilled lover.

The doors opened, and he practically drug her down the hall. This was her floor, their floor. He was taking her to his office. At least they could lock the door without worrying about anyone with a key showing up to interrupt them. Only he didn't turn right at the end of the hall like he should have. He turned left instead and pulled her into Mr. Greene's office.

"I've always wanted to do something in here as my way of saying fuck you to the asshole. You in?"

"Yes," Bethany sang out. She clamped her mouth over his. It was already starting to hurt her throat keeping up with the high pitched voice. The less talking she had to do the better.

She could feel his hands reaching for the zipper on the back of the dress, so she broke away from him. "Don't," she said, shaking her head. "It's a pain."

She slid her ass onto her boss's desk and spread her legs wide, pulling up her dress as she did so to show Billy there was nothing underneath save for her hot and ready box.

He licked his lips and grinned. "I like a woman who's prepared." He dropped to his knees in front of her and buried his face into her pussy.

It occurred to her briefly he hadn't asked for her name. There hadn't been the slightest hint he knew who she was or even cared to know who she was. The old Bethany would've been insulted enough to be turned off. This Bethany forgot what she was thinking about the moment his tongue brushed over her clit.

His tongue was like magic darting in and out of her tunnel, and he switched it up by sucking on her clit. Bethany tilted her head back and closed her eyes. She managed to find a chair with one foot to support herself and thrust into him, fucking his face while he ate her out. This was too good to be true. No one would ever believe Billy went down on her on Mr. Greene's desk at the Christmas party. It was hard to believe herself.

She came right away, more from the shock and utter personal joy of who was on his knees in front of her. The second orgasm took a bit more effort. Billy inserted one finger into her then two. He fucked her with his hand while his mouth claimed her clit. She bucked into his face, encouraging him until she was just at the height of her next climax. Her foot slipped off the chair and shook uncontrollably unable to find the floor for support.

The concept of time was lost. She had no idea how long they had been there. It could've been thirty seconds or thirty minutes. The party had no more than an hour left, so they couldn't spend as much time devouring each other as she would've liked.

When her orgasm subsided, she gently pushed him away from her and slid off the desk. He pouted and tried to object, but she won out. Once both of her feet were on the floor again, she spun around and lifted the back of her dress exposing her bare ass to him.

The mask had slipped on her face, but she couldn't straighten it without dropping the mounds of material she was holding. He was behind her anyway, so there wasn't much for her to look at. She could hear the sound of his zipper, and his slacks fell to the floor. He grabbed either side of her hips with his hands and gently moved her feet apart.

'I can't believe it,' she thought. *I'm really about to be fucked by the hottest guy at work.'*

She felt him position himself and begin to enter her. Then that was it. He was thrusting hard into her from behind. It caught her by such surprise it took a minute for her to realize she should be moaning. She leaned over the desk farther and tried to angle her hips for better reach while crying out how much she loved his cock. Nothing was working.

Billy wasn't the smallest cock she'd ever fucked, but in her fantasies, he was hung like a horse. She hadn't been expecting the short end of average.

Finally, they got into a good groove. He was the perfect size and at just the right angle to hit her g-spot. In seconds, she was crying out and wasn't faking it anymore. Her tunnel constricted around and tried to hold him in every time he pulled back to thrust into her again. The orgasm kept flowing for as long as he hit her g-spot. This was more like it. This was exactly how sex with Billy, the office God, was supposed to feel.

The party, the office, the fact they were in Mr. Greene's office, all of it had drifted away. The only things left in the world was her and Billy. Even the thoughts of how she was going to make a clean getaway had escaped her. Nothing could ruin this moment. They were so engrossed in their one night stand that neither of them heard the key turning in the lock.

The door opened, but they didn't notice that either. What finally caught their attention was the sound of Mr. Greene's angry voice. "What the hell are you doing in here?"

Bethany turned toward the door, but the mask was still askew on her face. She couldn't see anything except a blur. It didn't matter. Bethany could recognize her boss's voice anywhere.

"Get out!" He screamed and grabbed Billy pushing him toward the door.

Billy shuffled with his pants around his ankles, nearly falling twice. Trying to pull them up only slowed him down which made Mr. Greene even more irate, and he shoved at Billy harder. Their voices continued in the hallway. Mr. Greene was ordering him to leave immediately while Billy apologized profusely. The tone of his voice raised each time, and it sounded like he was close to crying.

'I wonder if he'll ask about his bonus,' Bethany giggled. She clasped her hand over her mouth and yanked her dress down around her legs, not caring if she was fully covered. The mask was more important, and she adjusted it. She couldn't flee if she couldn't see. If anyone could tell she just got laid during the office party, she didn't care. She needed to dash out while Mr. Greene was distracted.

She took two steps toward the door when her boss appeared. "Where do you think you're going?" he demanded, slamming the door shut behind him. He stood in front of her, rolling up his sleeves.

Bethany backed up until she hit the desk again. Mr. Greene was well known for his temper, but she'd never seen him this angry. His nostrils flared, and she thought it was cute how he looked when he was mad.

'Where did that come from?' she wondered. Mr. Greene was not someone she'd consider attractive. His green eyes were his best feature. His dark hair was always cut too short, and he was in a perpetual state of being "this" close to losing his top. Everyone walked on eggshells around him.

Bethany just stood there, waiting for her identity to be discovered. Any second now he'd ask her to remove the mask.

Then he dropped his arms and looked at her like she was the most desirable woman in the world. *'Oh, no,'* she thought. *'He's married.'* She had never considered herself the type who would sleep with a married man. The evening was getting worse by the second.

"I've wanted this for a long time, Brenda," he said, closing the distance between him.

'He thinks I'm the girl from Accounting.' Bethany was relieved,

but it was quickly replaced by the thumping of her heart beat in her clit. *'I am not turned on by this,'* she tried to convince herself.

"You have no idea how many days I've fantasized about bending you over my desk. Then I find you in here with that waste of space."

Her clit ached louder and stronger. It was turning her on. The ball. The mask. Being mistaken for someone else. Two men in one night. One was hot as hell, and this one was owning the situation. She was on the edge of climax already.

"What should I do with you?" he sneered.

It was a question he didn't expect her to answer. His lips covered hers, and he gripped her arms almost painfully tight, pulling her close. It caught her by surprise, and as soon as she melted into it, letting go of the last reservations she had of sleeping with her boss, he spun her around, pushing hard on her back until she laid flat over the desk.

He had his pants down and her dress up in record time. There was no foreplay or fumbling like there had been with Billy. Mr. Greene was a man who saw what he wanted and took it.

When he entered her, the cry of delight was real. His stiff cock spread her wide open. He yanked on her hips, pulling her to him with every powerful thrust, and it was still difficult to force his way into her tight tunnel.

"Brace yourself," he grunted.

Bethany was almost to her next orgasm, but took his warning to mean he was about to shoot his load. It was faster than she expected, but he was at least twice her age.

"You need to be punished," he told her. His hand came down across one of her cheeks hard, and she stifled a scream. It hurt like hell, but caused the gates to open. Her hot juices flowed down her tunnel, coating his balls as her labyrinth convulsed around his cock.

"And I'm an ass man," he said, pulling all the way out. He rammed his shaft into her tight backdoor quickly, and she tried to fly over the desk. His strong hands still gripped her waist and held her in place.

It took three hard, painful thrusts for his entire cock to enter her ass. Bethany's eyes watered from the brunt force of it. This wasn't the first time her ass had been fucked, but it had never been violated like this. Her body betrayed her. The shaking of her legs, the constricting of her tunnel, and her cum ran down her legs. All of it was proof of how much her body enjoyed it.

Mr. Greene began to moan, and he slowed his rhythm, making long thrusts all the way in and out. He was close. He pulled out, and she felt his cum shoot onto her ass. When he was finished, he rubbed it into her skin then smacked her ass again even harder.

Bethany stood up and straightened her dress. She took her time with it, not sure how to face her boss again. When she finally turned around, he was gone. *I guess he didn't want to face the awkwardness either.*

She grabbed her clutch from where she had dropped it on the chair. Laying on it was an envelope with her name written in her boss' handwriting. It was her bonus check. *Brenda, my ass,* she chuckled. *He knew exactly who he was fucking.*

She looked both ways down the hall before walking to the elevator. It was going to be unnerving at work for a while, but that was a Monday problem. The more pressing concern was sitting on her sore ass for the drive home.

Chapter Eight

Thursday

Tiff called bright and early Thursday morning at half past illegal o'clock. It wasn't often Bethany had a chance to sleep in, and it was even more rare she needed the rest after a glorious night of sex. This week being the exception to that. She groaned when the ringing of the phone interrupted her dream causing her eyes to open. She cursed when she saw her friend's name on the screen and sent it to voice mail.

As soon as she rolled over and got comfortable again, her phone rang a second time. Bethany threw the covers off her, trying to kick herself free, but got her foot caught in them. "What?" she asked angrily when she answered.

"Good morning to you too, sunshine," Tiff sang out.

"It's too early for this," Bethany moaned.

"Understand, but I need a favor."

"What?" Bethany expected there to be some necessary ingredient she needed to pick up on the way to dinner. It was typical Tiff. She's the only person who could plan a Thanksgiving meal, but forget to buy a turkey.

"Brad's friend Jimmy is coming to dinner. They were college roommates."

"Yeah." Bethany put the phone on mute and sat carefully on the toilet. Her ass was still sore from last night. Tiff was lucky she didn't make her listen. Served her right for waking her up.

"It was unexpected. We had invited him months ago, but he was going to visit his fiancé's family for the holiday."

Bethany was listening, but kept the phone on mute while she brushed her teeth.

"Anyway, they broke up."

She rolled her eyes. *'Oh, boo-hoo. Poor Johnny, or Jimmy, or whoever the hell he is.'*

"So he decided to come after all, but I was not made aware of this until this morning."

Bethany unmuted herself. "So wha?" she asked. The toothbrush hanging out of her mouth. "Nee me ta ge som-in?"

"What? No. Well, yes, actually I do."

She spit into the sink and filled a glass with water to rinse her mouth.

"I was hoping you wouldn't mind picking up Jimmy from the airport."

Bethany spit the water out involuntarily after hearing the unexpected request. It sprayed a foamy mix of toothpaste all over her mirror. "What?"

"I know! It's a lot. It's just that Brad's parents are here, and I'm cooking."

"So?" Bethany wiped at her mirror, feeling like her holiday was already ruined.

"So if Brad goes to get him, I'll have to deal with his mother. Alone. Without any defense."

Bethany rolled her eyes. There was one good thing about being single. She didn't have to deal with in-laws who could never accept anyone was good enough for their son.

"Well?" Tiff asked quietly.

"Fine. But you owe me."

"Yes! Thank you so much. And you're right. I owe you big. I'll have Brad text the flight details."

They hung up and Bethany got in the shower. Might as well let the spray of the water help wake her up. When she got out, she looked over the text for Brad. *'Shit. I should've gone straight there and skipped the shower. He's going to be waiting on me.'*

She got ready in record time, and as she ran through her apartment to leave, she thought about grabbing the love potion. *'Nah,'* she decided. *'I don't need to risk Brad going crazy over me.'*

An hour of intense driving later, she pulled up at the airport. Jimmy was waiting outside. Brad had been keeping him updated on her ETA and gave him a description of her car. She opened her door and stood up with one foot still inside. "Jimmy," she waved.

"I thought that might be you." He loaded his suitcase in the backseat and climbed in the passenger side. "Thank you so much for doing this."

"Anytime," she said. Bethany made a mental note to discuss a few things with Tiff later. She had sent a picture of Jimmy, but it had to be an old one from his early college days. The picture was of a grown boy, but there was a man sitting beside her in the car. A fine man at that. He had lost his puffy baby fat cheeks, and a chiseled jaw took their place. She regretted not grabbing her clutch which still contained the potion, but she couldn't use it. If she drank it now, they wouldn't make it to dinner.

Jimmy made polite conversation the entire drive. He talked about his school days with Brad and his job. He asked Bethany about herself then spent the rest of the drive discussing sports. Bethany simply nodded and acted like she understood what he was saying.

She was far from an expert on men, but she was certain of one thing. Jimmy was nice and extraordinarily friendly, but he was not interested in her at all. Whether it was because of his recent break up or because he didn't find her attractive, she couldn't be sure, but she chose to believe the former. It was a shame. This was how love was supposed to happen: naturally by circumstance, not forced by whatever the old witch crammed into that bottle.

There were still hours left until dinner was ready when they arrived. Jimmy joined Brad and his father in the living room watching the game. Bethany stuck close to Tiff shielding her from her mother-in-law. The woman adored Bethany. For every critique she gave Tiff, she followed it with two compliments towards Bethany. It was a ruse. They'd done this song and dance before with the moms of past boyfriends. She didn't really like Bethany all that much, but she wasn't dating her son which is what she liked about her. That, and complimenting Bethany was just another dig at Tiff.

Whenever possible, Bethany stole a glance at Jimmy. She could see the outline of his muscular chest beneath his shirt. The tight jeans he wore gave away everything she needed to know about him. As soon as dinner was over, Brad talked about running him to his motel.

"Don't worry about it," Bethany smiled. "I'll do it. Stay here and visit with your folks."

From the corner of her eye, she saw Tiff raise an eyebrow at her. If she knew what Bethany was up to, she didn't say a word to stop her.

"Do you mind if I run by my apartment real quick?" she asked Jimmy. "It's on the way, and I just need to run in and grab something."

He shook his head. "I'm at your mercy."

Bethany was thankful he didn't press the subject and ask what she needed. She didn't have a fake reason ready. A few minutes later, she pulled up in front of her building. "Two minutes," she told him and ran up the steps.

The clutch was on the chair in her bedroom. She grabbed the bottle and took a small swig as she walked back through her apartment. The smell alone was enough to invoke her gag reflexes. She grabbed a bottle of juice from the fridge and gulped it down until it started to drip from her mouth. She belched loudly and wondered if Jimmy would still find her attractive if he had heard her.

She put everything away and wiped off her face. Taking a few deep breaths to relax, she left and joined Jimmy back in her car. She put it in drive without looking at him and drove toward the motel where he reserved a room.

A couple blocks away, she felt him staring at her. When she turned, his eyes were filled with desire. *'Damn. I really do need to buy this stuff by the gallon.'*

"I have been wanting to be alone with you all day," he said.

It was hard for Bethany not to laugh at this point. He barely noticed she was there, forgot her name three times, and once looked at her surprised like he didn't realize she hadn't left after dropping him off. This wasn't really Jimmy speaking. It was the potion talking.

She almost felt bad about it. She had been tricking people into sleeping with her all week, but hadn't made that connection until now. By the time they arrived at the motel, she convinced herself it was no different than leaving a bar with someone when they're drunk. Everyone has one night stands they regret at some point.

Bethany pulled up front and waited for him to get his key. She drove him around the back of the motel near his room. "Wanna come up for..." he struggled, realizing he had nothing to offer.

"Sure," she said, not making him work for it.

She walked halfway across the room and waited for him to shut and lock the door. Then he headed straight toward her. She took control of the situation from the start. Nothing was going near her ass tonight.

They were on each other like lust crazed teenagers who had the house to themselves for twenty minutes before her mom got home from work. There was no time to spare. Her phone was vibrating in her purse, and she knew it was Tiff checking to see that she made it home okay. *More like checking to see if I went home.* She'd figure it out soon enough.

They stripped, and she pushed him back on the bed, climbing on top of him. She positioned herself over his beefy member, and helped guide his tip inside of her.

"No foreplay?" He looked at her surprised.

She shook her head. "I've been waiting to get you alone all night too. I'm ready."

Bethany lowered her hips slowly and allowed his cock to slide inside her. Her pussy ached from getting more action in a week than she was used to getting in a month if not more. Her ass cried out reminding her it was still tender. All of her body's complaints soon subsided as her pleasure grew.

Jimmy gave Billy a run for his money in the looks department, but he was far more endowed than her co-worker, making him the hottest guy she'd ever fucked. She was going to savor it for a moment.

When she lifted up, she let him slide almost all the way, but stopped at the tip then came down hard. She leaned forward, grabbing the headboard for support and fucked him hard and fast. Her first climax was already peaking.

"Oh, fuck, Beth!" Jimmy moaned. "Damn, girl. Your pussy is so fucking amazing."

"Bethany," she scolded him. Only her mom called her Beth, and that wasn't who she wanted to be thinking about during sex.

"Yes, Bethany, fuck me" he cried out.

She listened and did as she was told. She threw out everything she had ever learned about sex and fucked him in a way which pleased her until she was exhausted from multiple orgasms. She was about to concede, to slide off him and give him the lead when he finally came.

As soon as he was spent, she rolled off of him and cleaned herself up in the bathroom. When she came out, he was laying on his side in the bed, rubbing the spot next to him with gentle circles. He wanted her to join him again.

"Well, I have to get home," she said, grabbing her clothes off the floor.

"What?"

She got one leg in her pants before he was next to her.

"You can't stay?"

"No, I have work in the morning," she lied.

"Tomorrow? You don't have it off."

Bethany stood and fastened her jeans. "Not everyone has a four day weekend." That was the truth, but she happened to be one of those who did.

"It's fine. I can make sure you're up in time."

She stared at him dumbfounded. "Everything is at my apartment. My clothes. My work badge. Makeup. I have to go."

"Please stay," he insisted.

Jimmy continued to plead with her, but she ignored him. She continued to dress and was looking around for her other shoe when she thought she heard a whimper.

When she looked, he was sitting on the bed. His lower lip quivered.

'You've got to be fucking kidding me.'

"Did I do something wrong?" he asked.

"No."

"Don't you like me?"

"Yes. I guess. I mean this was fun, but I don't know you."

"So stay," he said, coming to her again. "We can get to know each other better."

'Is this how I look when I'm getting dumped and trying to ask why he's ending it? It's disgusting.'

"I can't Jimmy. I have to go." She grabbed her shoes and went outside, putting them on just before heading down the stairs. There was the sound of a door closing, and she took off, afraid he had thrown on some clothes to come after her.

Bethany peeled out of the lot and kept looking back. Even when she parked at her building, she checked all her mirrors worried he had somehow managed to keep up with her.

Chapter Nine

Friday

At some point, Brad gave Jimmy her number. He sent her a text letting her know and gave her Jimmy's number as well. "I'm sick of hearing him whine about you, so you deal with him," the text said. She knew the potion would wear off, and he'd leave her alone. It wasn't losing its power over him quick enough, so she blocked him shortly after returning home last night.

Tiff wasn't happy with her, but hadn't said too much. Jimmy had hoped to work things out with his fiancé, so sleeping with her caused him a lot of guilt he'd have to work through. He was beside himself over whether or not to tell his ex about what happened. It seemed like Tiff was hell bent on passing Jimmy's guilt onto her.

The morning started out slow. Bethany had made the decision before bed not to use the potion today. There was only enough for one more time at the most as it was. When she woke up, she was still determined to take a day off from men. She was exhausted and needed the rest. Plus her insight last night to how she was taking advantage of them still wasn't sitting well with her.

Then she checked the mail.

The postcard featuring the psychic's home on the front wouldn't have surprised her. She had filled out a line in a guest book, giving the woman her address when she was there. A special holiday sale was being promoted. The edges read, "Show this card for 50% off any reading, or any one item in the shop."

It was when she flipped the card over she gasped. Written by hand on the back was a note. "Not valid on any potions. Come in for a reading."

Something told her she really should listen to the old woman. She got dressed and drove there. The parking area was empty except for one car which she assumed belonged to the witch. She opened the side door to the porch, and the inside door opened immediately.

"I told you a couple of drops, not to do shots with it," Max glared at her.

Bethany could barely meet her eyes. She said, "Hi," quietly, and shuffled past her into the room.

"You've been having fun, haven't you?" Max didn't wait for an answer. "I can tell by the way you're walking."

Bethany hadn't come here to be humiliated. She was debating whether or not she should leave.

"I kid," the old woman said. "Sit."

The woman laid the Tarot deck on the table then stared at Bethany. "Payment up front."

I can't believe I'm doing this.' She fished the cash from her purse.

"Let me guess. You're still looking for love even after all the affection you've had."

"You know," Bethany said, standing up. "Maybe I should go."

"Sit," Max ordered. She shuffled and dealt out the cards. "It was too much. I warned you of that. How will you know a man's true intentions if you cloud his thoughts too much? Huh?"

Bethany sat back down, but kept her eyes glued to the cards

as if she could understand what they meant on her own. Max was irritated with her. She wasn't too happy with herself either.

"Oh," Max laughed. "This is good."

"What?" Bethany leaned closer.

"It appears you have met your soul mate since you were last here after all."

"I did?" Bethany would've been in disbelief, but Max had proven herself and her abilities completely.

Max nodded. "Mmm-hmm. It would seem he misses you and longs to see you again."

"Who is he?"

"Too many to track?" Max snapped at her.

Bethany dropped her hands in her lap, and her shoulders slumped. She stared at all the vials in the shop for sale. Many of them were decorative, and she found herself wishing she'd never picked up the bottle of love potion.

"If you'd been using it right, you'd have recognized love when you found it. I said a couple of drops at a time, not a fraction of the bottle."

"I know," Bethany said defensively. Then repeated the words more calmly, "I know. What now? There were only attracted to me because of the potion. There's no guarantee they'll still want me."

"Oh, but he will. The one whose heart is true still wants you."

"How can I figure out which one he is?" Bethany hated the words coming out of her mouth, but there was no one but herself to blame.

"There are quite a few for you to shuffle through, aren't there? I'm sorry. I don't see who it is. I can't tell you. All I can say is he will still be interested in you without the love potion."

"So what? I should track them all down and see which one is happy to see me?"

Max rocked her head from side to side in thought. "Something like that. Yes, that will work."

Bethany sighed and stared at the cards. The pictures painted on them made it look like a kid's deck. They would almost match next to each other on a shelf: Old Maid, Go Fish, and Tarot.

"And what about the others?" she asked.

"Hmm?" Max's eyebrows narrowed at her.

"The ones who aren't my soul mate. How will they react to me?"

Max shrugged, "Well, that would depend on how you affected them as well. Some may be hurt. Some may be indifferent."

Bethany nodded and chewed the inside of her cheek. *'I suppose I deserve that.'*

"Yes, you do," Max spat, reading her mind.

Bethany drove home dreading what she had to do next. There had to be an easier way. Tracking down some of these guys would be hard enough. That didn't even take into consideration how much she didn't want to. If she knew which one was her soul mate, it'd be easy. She didn't want to have a string of figurative doors slammed in her face while she tried to figure out who he was though.

Bethany thought about the week she had, trying to remember the details of everyone she met. Mark was an easy one to cross off the list. He could get ahold of her. She might have his number blocked, but he knew where she lived, where she worked, and how to bother her friends. If he was pining for her, she'd have heard by now. There was no way he was her soul mate, and if he was, she'd rather stay single.

"Who else can I check off my list without leaving my house again tonight?" She asked to her empty apartment.

The roommates didn't give her a number, nor did Adam or the guy at the bar. "There's Bruce," she said, opening her laptop. She had already deleted his number from her phone, but they had met online.

She went to the website and searched through her messages. There were a lot of new ones since she'd last been on the site. Bruce's messages seemed to have disappeared. She scanned over the list a few different times without seeing his picture or name. Making one more attempt, she looked at each one carefully, even opening the messages in case he changed his profile picture and his user name.

Some of the profile pictures were clearly not him, but people have done weirder stuff. Finally, she found him. There was no picture available, and his handle simply read, "User." There were a string of messages after she bailed on him at the bookstore. He was asking where she was and what he had done wrong. One even professed his love for her. The messages ended around the time the effects of the potion would've worn off. The very last item on the list was an account message in bold type, **"Profile has been blocked by User."**

Bethany leaned back and sighed. *'Doesn't look like it's him. He would've unblocked me by now if nothing else.'*

The first two she crossed off the list weren't even definite no's. They were likely assumptions. This could take a lot longer than she expected.

Billy and Mr. Greene she'd have to face on Monday as much as she was dreading it. They both had access to the company directory which meant they could call or email her if they wanted. *'I know it's not Mr. Greene. He's married regardless of if it's happily or not. Billy is unlikely too. The women he dates belong on a magazine cover. Besides, he's never shown interest in me until the party.'* She was going to leave them alone for now too. If she made her way through the rest of the list without success, she'd approach them at work.

It was pretty discouraging. Even with the knowledge that one of them wanted to see her again, was hoping to see her again, the list was dwindling fast. The only other one she could contact from home was Jimmy.

"Tiffany's already irritated with me," she said, talking to herself again. "Oh, well. Might as well rip off the Band-Aid."

She exhaled slowly while blowing the air between her lips making a long raspberry sound and scrolled through her phone. It took a minute to find the blocked number list in her settings. The phone made it much easier to block then unblock. She wrote down the top one listed on a scratch sheet of paper then called it. It rang twice before it connected. "Hello," a male voice said hesitantly.

"Hi, Jimmy?"

"Yes."

"It's Bethany. Tiff's friend."

Click. The line went dead. She pulled the phone from her ear and stared at the screen.

"Well," she said. "I guess that answers that question."

There were only three left, technically five. The college guys who shared an apartment were unlikely. Bethany wasn't anywhere near old yet, but compared to them she felt like an old lady. None of them were probably her true love. There were also the guys she met at the bar and the beach.

'Wonder what I'd do if it's the guy from the bar?' He was not her usual type at all. Of course, maybe that's why she had bad luck with men. She'd been fishing in the wrong ponds.

Adam was the guy from the beach, but she could barely remember what he looked like. She closed her eyes and tried to picture him from her memories, but every time, the sun was behind him shining brightly, blinding her and blocking her from seeing his face.

"Wait!" She jumped from the couch and ran to her bedroom. "He gave me his phone number."

Bethany was halfway to her room when she screeched on the brakes. The number had been tucked into her jacket. It was the same one she wore to dinner yesterday and had left at Tiff's house. She wondered how long she'd have to wait to get it back or to ask her friend to give her the number from her pocket. She wasn't sure, but she had a feeling today was too soon.

"Okay. We'll circle back to him too."

She freshened up and grabbed her things to leave. It would be the frat guys first then the bar. She'd save the beach for tomorrow. Maybe Tiff would call, and they'd be alright again to ask for the number. Otherwise, it was getting too late to head to the beach today.

Bethany drove around in circles near where the guys lived. She could remember exactly where Tiff had come to pick her up. The rest was a little hazy. It hadn't been too far from the apartment building, and she had to turn a corner to get to Tiff's car. There was a partial border wall along the walkway to the building and some decorative large potted plants in barrels out front. She finally thought she saw it, but she was going in the wrong direction. She kept driving the block in the way she left the building, but she needed to see the way it looked when she pulled up to it like she had with Levi. Once she made the quick turn around and came back, it was clear. This was the building.

Bethany didn't remember the building having a locked entrance, but she hadn't been the one who needed to open the door either. She looked at the names listed to buzz for entrance. It didn't help much. There were no first names on it, and she didn't know any of their last names. Several apartments had three names listed too, she couldn't narrow it down that way. She couldn't remember the apartment number, but she could get to it easily. Take the stairs up one flight, turn right, and it was the door straight down at the end of the hall.

In the movies, people always press a random button, and the person buzzes them in automatically. With her luck, she'd get the paranoid person who'd call the police on her once they realized she was a stranger trying to gain entrance. While she was standing there trying to decide her next move, a man walked up and unlocked the door.

She glanced at him and half smiled. To her surprise, he stood aside with the door open for her. "Thank you," she said, hurrying inside.

"Who are you visiting?" the man asked, heading to the wall of mailboxes.

"Levi," she said from the stairs.

"Oh, Levi. Good kid."

Bethany was already headed down the second floor hallway and couldn't hear if the man said anything else. Her heart was beating fast and fight or flight was kicking in from her nerves, but she had to get it over with already. She knocked on the door quickly and took a step back.

There was movement inside followed by the chain lock being removed. The door opened, only a crack at first then wider. It was either Wes or Jordan. She wasn't quite sure.

"Hi," she said.

"May I help you?"

'Great. He doesn't remember me. I hadn't expected that.'

"I was here the other day," Bethany began.

"Who is it?" a voice rang out from the apartment.

The guy at the door looked at her and raised his eyebrows like he was waiting for her to answer that question for him.

"I'm Bethany."

Nothing registered on his face. No recollection at all. "Bethany!" he shouted back.

"What does she want?" the third guy asked, walking to the door.

'Okay. I think that means two down. Now I just need to find out how the third feels about me.'

She wouldn't have to wait long. The other two came to the door. "Need something," Levi asked. The voice matched with the guy who'd asked for her name.

"Sorry to bother you," she said. "Did I leave my jacket here? I had something important in the pocket."

"Who are you again?" the third guy asked.

"Bethany," she repeated.

"I don't think you were wearing one," Levi told her.

"Okay. Thank you," she said.

As the door shut, she saw the third guy remark. "That's Bethany? *The* Bethany? Can't be. Bethany was a goddess not a frumpy middle aged woman like her."

'Ouch.'

She walked back to the car trying to talk herself out of going to the bar. There were only two options left. At this time on Friday night, the beach would be overrun with partiers. She doubted Adam would be there, and if he was, the chances of seeing him, or him seeing her, were slim. There was also no guarantee she'd have any luck at the bar.

'Donnie? Danny? It was a D name I'm almost positive.' If she was being honest, she probably wouldn't recognize him either. Bulky guy with a beard. Maybe.

Like it was on autopilot, the car drove her straight there. She sat in the parking lot for twenty minutes psyching herself up. Going out in public alone was one of her biggest anxiety triggers. She was not a social person without the moral support provided from being with friends. Or, the help of a witch's brew.

People do it all the time. The worst that could happen is someone else hits on her. She could do what she wants with that. It might even be a little empowering to see she was attractive without the use of the potion even if it was someone who'd been drinking who made a move.

'No, the worst that could happen is no one approaches me because not even drunks think I look good.'

She finally forced herself to walk inside and sit at the bar. She'd have one beer. If nothing happened by the time she drank it, she'd go home and regroup. When she glanced around, she didn't see anybody who looked familiar. If the guy she met was here, and if he was the one the psychic was talking about, he'd come to her.

When she set the empty bottle on the counter, a man approached her. He was handsome with crystal clear blue eyes and blonde hair. He wasn't the one she had a fling with in the alley. "Can I buy you a drink?"

"No, thank you. I'm leaving."

"So soon?" he laughed.

"Yeah, the friend I was supposed to meet sent a message saying there was a change of plans."

It made her feel a little better as she walked to the car, but she was no closer to figuring out if the bar guy was the one she was supposed to find. Either he was there and he didn't recognize her which meant he wasn't the one, or she still had to track him down.

When she returned to her apartment, she went over her list again. Tomorrow she'd go to the beach looking for Adam. She'd look for him again on Sunday if she had to since that was the day she ran into him there. Unless she heard from Tiff and got the number from her jacket pocket before then. She was going to wait until Tiff was ready to talk

On Monday, she'd know for sure about Billy and Mr. Greene. She could keep trying at the bar until Danny – *pretty sure its Danny* – came to her, or until she saw someone who hopefully triggered the memory of what he looked like to know if it was him or not.

It would only leave Mark if none of that worked. If that was the case, she'd just buy a bunch of cats.

Chapter Ten

Saturday

This was it. Bethany was walking a fine line between happily ever after and crazy cat lady. She pulled up to the beach mid-morning and looked around. It wasn't empty. There were more families than she expected. It was a lot busier than last Sunday when, she assumed, most of these people would've been sitting in church.

She wandered around the beach aimlessly for a while, but didn't see anyone vaguely familiar who would fit his profile. She couldn't remember his face clearly, but his build was unforgettable. Everywhere she looked, she only saw couples and families. There were no single men in sight.

'Alright, he was jogging this way when I first ran into him, and he left his stuff down by that secluded area.'

She went to where they had sex on the beach, and a familiar throbbing began in her clit like her body recognized the area too. Then she turned and walked along the shoreline, scouring the faces of everyone she passed. He wasn't here.

Well beyond the stairs leading to the parking lot, she finally stopped. If he was a habitual runner, he'd be here tomorrow. She'd come back and try again. When she turned to head back to the stairs, she saw him.

Adam was jogging down the beach toward her. He didn't notice her at first, but once he did, he veered off from his path just enough to come straight to her. "Hi," he said.

Bethany smiled, and said the first thing to pop in her head. "I lost your number."

'That doesn't make me sound desperate at all,' she thought. Her plan hadn't been to admit she came to the beach looking for him, but to play it off like it was another casual encounter again.

He glanced up toward the stairs. "I was just finishing up. Want to get lunch?"

She nodded, not wanting to open her mouth and say something else that would embarrass her.

"I'll grab my stuff. Meet you at the top?"

"Okay," she said.

This was promising, but it wasn't a guarantee. He could be willing to fuck her again or even date her without thinking she was the woman of his dreams. It was a topic she wasn't sure how to bring up. 'Hey, you haven't been sitting around miserable without me, have you?' didn't seem like the way to go.

He made it to the parking lot and waved at her, walking to his car. She followed him and waited while he loaded his bag in the trunk. He closed the lid and wiped his face off with a towel. "Where would you like to eat?"

"Your place."

There was a sudden look of surprise on his face which melted into a warm and sexy stare. He wrapped one arm behind her, pulling her close. "I hope you're on the special," he said, leaning in for a kiss.

They wasted no time in driving to his house and were ripping each other's clothes off before the front door shut completely. He walked her backward to the couch until her knees hit the arm and buckled. He gently pressed her back and she fell on the couch with her legs hanging over the side.

Adam removed her panties and knelt on the floor. He buried his face between her legs, circling them with his arms and lifting her into the position he wanted. His tongue found her clit and teased it gently until she warmed up. He brought one arm down and moved his hand between her legs, fingering her first with one finger then two. His tongue continued to lap at her clit, and he'd lower his face to tongue fuck her labyrinth then return to the sweet spot.

She found it hard to find traction. She desperately wanted to buck her hips into his face, to show him how good it felt, but she wasn't able. Her moans grew and soon she climaxed, forgetting completely about the potion or if this was her soul mate. The only thing on her mind was cramming his cock into her tunnel.

Adam stood up and pulled her ass up on the arm of the couch. He nudged her legs apart with his knees and bent slightly to align his shaft with her entrance. He pressed into her, and she moaned low and soft. His cock felt amazing filling her.

He started off slow and steady, building a regular rhythm. At the angle her hips were arched, he hit her g-spot with every stroke. Six strokes in, and she could feel her tunnel constrict around him. Two minutes later, her legs were shaking uncontrollably, and she was exhausted.

He built up the tempo, fucking her in faster, harder strokes. One long continuous orgasm rocked through her body sending shockwaves to her nerves all over her body. Her juices flowed over out and over his cock. The last few thrusts were deep, and he grinded against her before pulling back to drive into her again. Then he collapsed on top of her while his cum filled her with warmth.

Her eyes were closed, and she tried to steady her breathing. She didn't see him when he moved up on the couch, taking her with him. They lay side by side, basking in their climax.

She glanced back at him and caught his eye which made her smile. She snuggled into him and could've easily fallen asleep right there in his arms.

"I'm glad I ran into you today," he said.

"Me too."

"I had wondered why you didn't call, kicking myself for not getting your number. Is that why you came to the beach today? To find me?"

"Yes," she admitted. She didn't have the energy to think about whether she wanted to come clean or not.

Minutes passed in silence. They lay still listening to the sound of each other's heartbeat as they slowed back to normal.

"Bethany," he said.

"Mmm-hmm," she was almost out.

"I don't want to scare you away."

"You won't," she mumbled.

Adam laughed nervously. "No, I mean I was hoping to see you again. I haven't been able to stop thinking about you. I felt like we had a connection, like I've known you my whole life even though we had only just met."

Bethany's eyes opened, and she looked down at his hand firmly placed on her abdomen. It was his left hand. The hand which would one day sport a gold band. This was him. This was the man she'd been trying to find.

More by Darling Coxx
The Nanny Diaries Series
The Family Secrets Series
Supernatural Erotica Series
True Love's Kiss
Nightstalker
Love Potion Number 9
Deadly Sins
Pride
Greed
Lust
Spring Break Affairs Series
Obeying Orders Series

About the Author

Darling Coxx is a seasoned writer who has been featured in many major publications under her given name. Taking a break from interviews and personal experience pieces, she is trying her hand at short novellas in the same genre she's been working in for most of her life.

Her adult entertainment career began while working as the manager of an adult store. It is her favorite position of any she's held, before or since. It was there where she made the contacts that allowed her to venture into the world of adult entertainment both in her own writing as well as producing a few pieces of her own.

Please feel free to reach out to her at DarlingCoxx@gmail.com. Follow her on Instagram @DarlingCoxx to stay updated on future publications.

www.ingramcontent.com/pod-product-compliance
Lightning Source LLC
Chambersburg PA
CBHW030843200726
48285CB00007B/2529